MY MAMA SAYS
THERE AREN'T ANY
ZOMBIES, GHOSTS, VAMPIRES,
CREATURES, DEMONS, MONSTERS,
FIENDS, GOBLINS, OR THINGS

MY MAMA SAYS
THERE AREN'T ANY
ZOMBIES, GHOSTS, VAMPIRES, CREATURES, DEMONS, MONSTERS,
FIENDS, GOBLINS, OR THINGS

Judith Viorst • *Drawings by Kay Chorao*

ALADDIN BOOKS
Macmillan Publishing Company
New York

Aladdin Books
Macmillan Publishing Company
866 Third Avenue, New York, NY 10022
Collier Macmillan Canada, Inc.

First Aladdin Books edition 1977
Second Aladdin Books edition 1988
Printed in the United States of America

A hardcover edition of My Mama Says There Aren't Any Zombies, Ghosts,
Vampires, Creatures, Demons, Monsters, Fiends, Goblins, or Things
is available from Atheneum Publishers, Macmillan Publishing Company.

10   9   8   7   6   5   4   3   2

Library of Congress Cataloging-in-Publication Data
Viorst, Judith.
My mama says there aren't any zombies, ghosts, vampires, creatures,
demons, monsters, fiends, goblins, or things.
Summary: If his mother has made other important
mistakes, can Nick trust her word that there are no
goblins and such lurking around in the night?
[1. Mothers—Fiction. 2. Monsters—Fiction]
I. Chorao, Kay, ill. II. Title.
PZ7.V816My 1988   [E]   87-18733
ISBN 0-689-71204-9

To my very own Nick,
who helped me write this book.

My mama says there isn't any mean-eyed monster
with long slimy hair and pointy claws
going scritchy-scratch, scritchy-scritchy-scratch
outside my window.

But yesterday my mama said
I couldn't have some cream cheese on my sandwich,
because, she said, there wasn't any more.

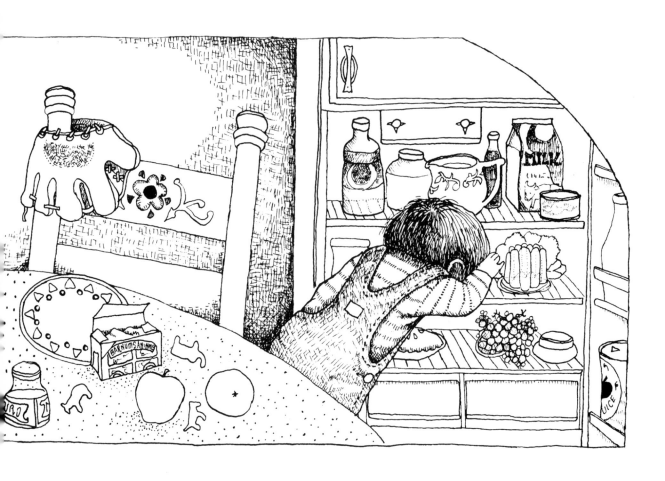

And then I found the cream cheese

under the lettuce

in back of the Jello. So…

sometimes even mamas make mistakes.

My mama says that a vampire
isn't flying over my house
with his red and black vampire cape
and his vampire f-f-f-fangs.

But how can I believe her

when she said my wriggly tooth would fall out Thursday,

and then it stayed till Sunday after lunch?

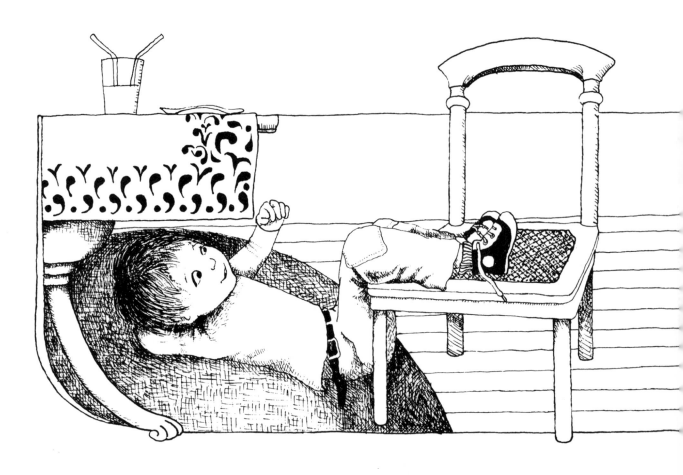

And once she gave me 19 cents
when yo-yos cost a quarter. So...
sometimes even mamas make mistakes.

On certain nights

when everyone's cozy and sleeping,

all of a sudden I hear a Thing in the yard.

And you know what it says as it ooooozes along?

It says, Nick, I am coming to get you.

My mama says it's positively not.

But when we shopped at the supermarket Friday,

my mama told me to carry the bag with the eggs.

It's heavy, I said, too heavy for me.

Oh, you can do it, she told me.

I can't.

You can.

I can't.

You can.

I can't.

You can, she told me.

And that's how there got to be scrambled eggs
all over my shoes.

And that lady. So…

sometimes even mamas make mistakes.

And sometimes in my bunk bed I start thinking,
maybe a fiend sneaked into my lower bunk.
And he's sniffing around for a boy to eat,
and I'm the boy that he's sniffing, and...
My mama says no fiends have sneaked in here.

But why did she scold me for leaving my skates
on the sidewalk?
Those were Anthony's skates.
I remembered to put mine away.

And once she said I hadn't flushed,
and it was Alexander's. So…
sometimes even mamas make mistakes.

My mama says that a tall white ghost
who goes "hoo!" from a hole in its mouth,
isn't hoo-hoo-hooing in my closet.

This morning, though, she made me wear my boots.
And then it didn't rain—or even drizzle.

And once I asked for chocolate nut
and she brought back rum raisin. So...
sometimes even mamas make mistakes.

My mama says that a zombi

with his eyes rolled back in his head,

and his arms out stiff,

and his skin as cold as ice,

isn't clonking up and up the stairs.

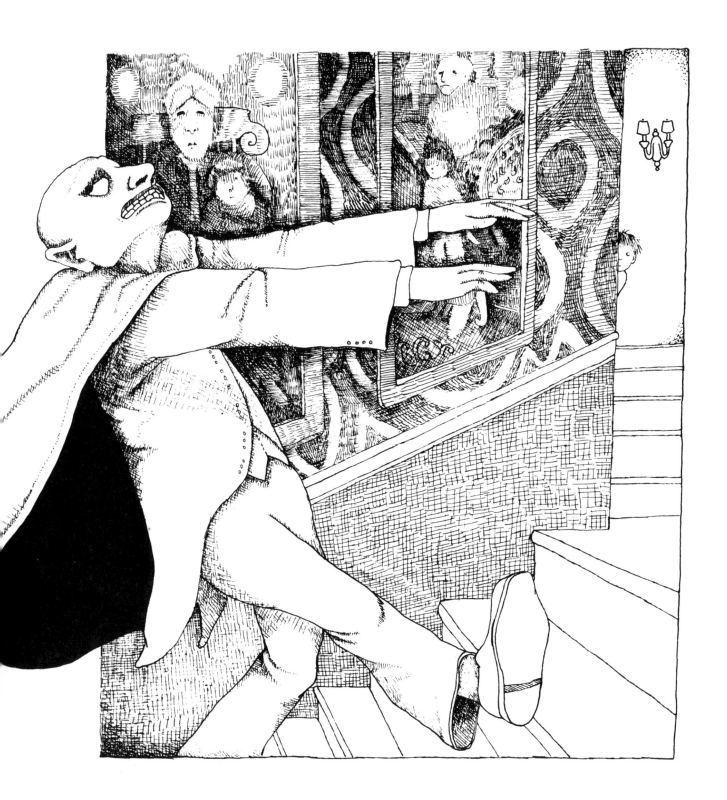

But how can I believe her
when she told me Holly's middle name was Susan.
And Holly's middle name is really Jane.

And once she said I wasn't
when I told her I was going to be car sick. So...
sometimes even mamas make mistakes.

And sometimes in the dark a demon

is switching his spidery tail.

And waiting.

Waiting for someone.

Who could it be?

And he's laughing a "heh!"

And a "hah!"

And a "hee!"

Which could give someone goose bumps in summer.

He isn't there, my mama says to me.

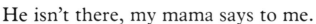

But how does she know

when she still doesn't know how to drive me

to Christopher's house without getting us lost on the way?

She tells me, Zip your jacket up.

But she can't zip it either. So...

sometimes even mamas make mistakes.

And I'm sure I've seen a goblin

slinking out of my dresser drawer

with a sack on his back to take me to goblin-y lands

where boys and girls eat brussels sprouts

and never get a birthday.

Oh, no, you haven't, Mama always says.

But Monday Mama said
she put my crayons on my shelf.
Just use your eyes, she said,
and you will find them.
I can't.
You can.
I can't.
You can.
I can't.

All right! *I'll* find them,

she said (not very nicely).

But, guess what?

She couldn't, too. So...

sometimes even mamas make mistakes.

My mama says that a creature

isn't reaching out his hand

to pinch me,

or squinch me,

or push me,

or squush me,

or—agggh!

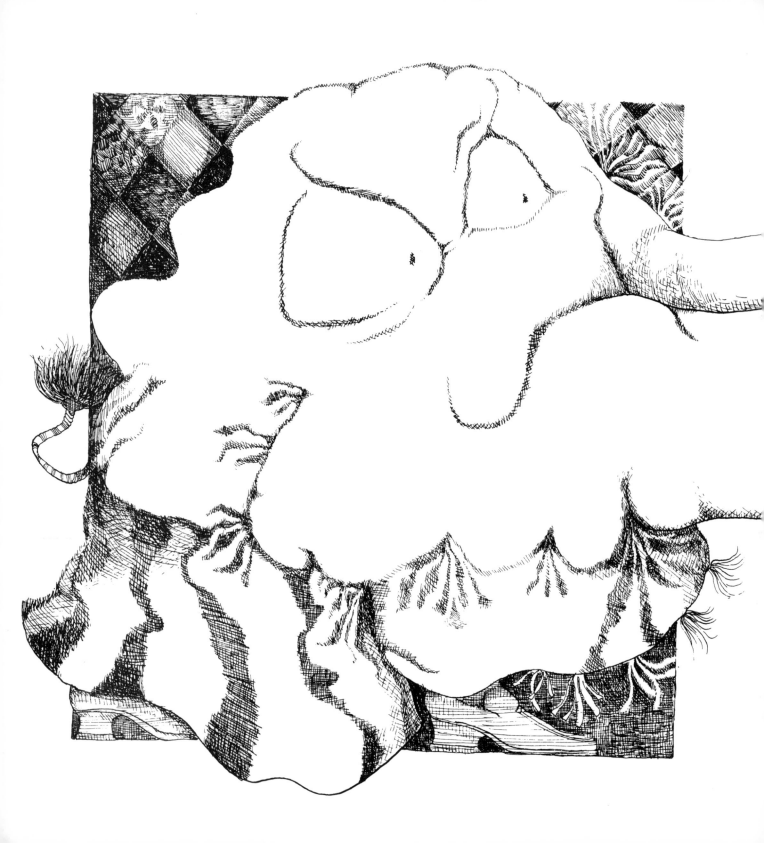

Well, sometimes even mamas make mistakes.

But sometimes they don't.

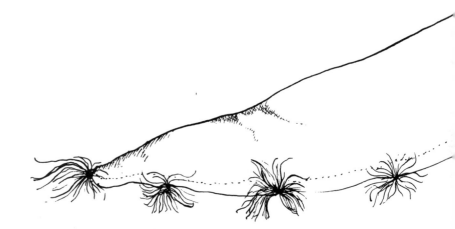